THE
Paper Bag
Princess

STORY BY
Robert Munsch

ART BY
Michael Martchenko

annick press
toronto • berkeley

Annick Press Ltd.

We acknowledge the support of the Canada Council for the Arts and the Ontario Arts Council, and the participation of the Government of Canada/la participation du gouvernement du Canada for our publishing activities.

Library and Archives Canada Cataloguing in Publication

Title: The paper bag princess / story by Robert Munsch ; art by Michael Martchenko.
Names: Munsch, Robert N., 1945- author. | Martchenko, Michael, illustrator.
Description: 40th anniversary edition.
Identifiers: Canadiana (print) 20190162821 | Canadiana (ebook) 20190162848 | ISBN 9781773213439
   (hardcover) | ISBN 9781773213842 (EPUB) | ISBN 9781773213866 (PDF) | ISBN 9781773213859 (Kindle)
Classification: LCC PS8576.U575 P36 2020 | DDC jC813/.54—dc23

Published in the U.S.A. by Annick Press (U.S.) Ltd.
Distributed in Canada by University of Toronto Press.
Distributed in the U.S.A. by Publishers Group West.

Printed in China

annickpress.com

robertmunsch.com

Also available as an e-book. Please visit annickpress.com/ebooks for more details.

A Note to Readers

For years, we read *The Paper Bag Princess* by Robert Munsch every single night. It was the last book before bedtime and it's hard for me to imagine a better one to help launch our children's dreams.

In this classic story, a dragon burns down Princess Elizabeth's castle, carries off her Prince Ronald, and leaves her with nothing save a paper bag and her own grit. Elizabeth quickly dons the paper bag and sets off to rescue Ronald. Her combination of courage, cleverness, and patience lead her to defeat the dragon and liberate Ronald. When Ronald shows no gratitude for Elizabeth's heroism and has the temerity to criticize her appearance, Elizabeth sheds no tears, tells Ronald what she thinks of him, and dances herself off into what is no doubt a very happily ever after.

We love reading this book as a family, sometimes even acting it out. I think it is critical that our daughter and sons and all our daughters and sons grow up to believe they can defeat their own dragons and rescue themselves. I think it is particularly important that girls and boys alike see determined, strong, and smart girls like Elizabeth doing so.

As our kids get older, *The Paper Bag Princess* is no longer a nightly ritual, though it remains a treasured part of our library. I will always be grateful for Elizabeth's bravery, and for the way she shows us that dragons can be defeated, that we can rescue ourselves, and that we don't need to sacrifice our kindness or goodness to do so.

Thank you, Robert Munsch.

Chelsea Clinton

Stand Up to Dragons

On my desk beside me is a slim, square book with yellowed pages, a copy of *The Paper Bag Princess*, by beloved children's author Robert Munsch.

Beautiful Elizabeth is about to marry Prince Ronald—a tousle-headed blond with a retroussé nose, a haughty air, and extremely snug trousers—when he is unexpectedly snatched by a dragon. Princess Elizabeth doesn't hesitate. She chases after the giant fire-breathing beast, outwits it with her cunning, and eventually liberates the prisoner. Ronald, still clutching his tennis racket, is less than impressed by her daring. She has lost her gown, messed up her hair, and she smells of ashes. How very unfeminine she was, to save his life.

Plucky Elizabeth is characteristically robust about the pettiness of her fiancé. "Ronald," she tells him, as uncowed and forthright as she was with the dragon, "your clothes are really pretty, and your hair is very neat. You look like a real prince, but you are a bum." Elizabeth tells it like it is. In the book's final illustration, she capers off towards the horizon and her own golden future beyond, arms raised into the sunset, dirty bare feet leaping joyfully in the dust. I recount this story in full because it was the most important book I ever read.

It is all but impossible to overstate the impact of this book upon my six-year-old self. It's true that in later life it didn't stop me waiting longer than I should have by a silent telephone, nor do I always speak my mind to men, nor defend myself as I ought against subtle sexist insult, derision, or plain bad manners. I struggle with the unwieldy ugliness of the word "mansplain" though it certainly helps make visible a phenomenon women have long instinctively recognized. Still, in the face of such encounters I am not always as robust as I would like.

But the book has always been there in my psyche, whispering softly, a second narrative interwoven with the blasting electronic symphonies of popular culture that declare through every billboard and magazine and movie and pop song and the sound system of every mall: Be pleasing! Be nice! Be fragrant! Be thin! Conform! Elizabeth stayed with me, whispered to me of another empowered femininity, warning me of Ronalds.

The Paper Bag Princess is on my desk today because I have small twin daughters, and I wanted—no, needed—to read it to them. Of course, the lesson of the book is for future Ronalds as well as future Elizabeths—I'd have dug it out for a son just as readily as for my girls. The moral then becomes one of respecting women, of judging what lies beyond the paper bag the princess was forced to wear when the dragon's breath burned her royal robes, of always speaking to a woman as to an equal or, if you don't, to rue the consequences.

That women are human is a lesson the world has been busily striving to forget of late, if indeed it ever learned it. But with such depressing devolution has come an unexpected consequence: revolution. New oxygen breathed into the women's movement. The uniting of disparate civil rights movements as the examination of repression and discrimination becomes increasingly intersectional. And the startling viral sweep of #MeToo across the world, launching a widespread, systematic process of examining (and one hopes in time dismantling) institutionalized sexual harassment on a scale previously unimaginable. Change will come, the world has shown us, when women raise their voices. When we find the courage to answer back.

How to parent daughters while living through a backslide into cronyism, pettiness, and institutionalized misogyny? I don't know, but this morning I searched my mother's basement for *The Paper Bag Princess*, and though my children are barely three years old, that is where I will begin. I will read it to them and I hope over time that they will learn Princess Elizabeth's lessons: Adventure and be fearless. Stand up to dragons. Defend yourself with all you have. Walk away from any man who treats you with disrespect. You, yourself, alone, are enough, and more than enough.

For now, at three years old, that will have to do. That, and to hear their mother saying aloud to any man (to anyone) who disrespects her—you are a bum. After which my girls and I will all hold hands and skip off—or march, as necessary—into the sunset.

Francesca Segal

An earlier version of this article appeared online on The Hairpin in February 2017

To Elizabeth

Elizabeth was a beautiful princess.

She lived in a castle and had expensive princess clothes.

She was going to marry a prince named Ronald.

Unfortunately, a dragon smashed her castle, burned all her clothes with his fiery breath, and carried off Prince Ronald.

Elizabeth decided to chase the dragon and get Ronald back.

She looked everywhere for something to wear, but the only thing she could find that was not burnt was a paper bag. So she put on the paper bag and followed the dragon.

He was easy to follow, because he left a trail of burnt forests and horses' bones.

Finally, Elizabeth came to a cave with a large door that had a huge knocker on it. She took hold of the knocker and banged on the door.

The dragon stuck his nose out of the door and said, "Well, a princess! I love to eat princesses, but I have already eaten a whole castle today. I am a very busy dragon. Come back tomorrow."

He slammed the door so fast that Elizabeth almost got her nose caught.

Elizabeth grabbed the knocker and banged on the door again.

The dragon stuck his nose out of the door and said, "Go away. I love to eat princesses, but I have already eaten a whole castle today. I am a very busy dragon. Come back tomorrow."

"Wait," shouted Elizabeth. "Is it true that you are the smartest and fiercest dragon in the whole world?"

"Yes," said the dragon.

"Is it true," said Elizabeth, "that you can burn up ten forests with your fiery breath?"

"Oh, yes," said the dragon, and he took a huge, deep breath and breathed out so much fire that he burned up fifty forests.

"Fantastic," said Elizabeth, and the dragon took another huge breath and breathed out so much fire that he burned up one hundred forests.

"Magnificent," said Elizabeth, and the dragon took another huge breath, but this time nothing came out. The dragon didn't even have enough fire left to cook a meatball.

Elizabeth said, "Dragon, is it true that you can fly around the world in just ten seconds?"

"Why, yes," said the dragon, and jumped up and flew all the way around the world in just ten seconds.

He was very tired when he got back, but Elizabeth shouted, "Fantastic, do it again!"

So the dragon jumped up and flew around the whole world in just twenty seconds.

When he got back he was too tired to talk, and he lay down and went straight to sleep.

Elizabeth whispered, very softly, "Hey, dragon."
The dragon didn't move at all.

She lifted up the dragon's ear and put her head right inside. She shouted as loud as she could, "Hey, dragon!"

The dragon was so tired he didn't even move.

Elizabeth walked right over the dragon and opened the door to the cave.

There was Prince Ronald. He looked at her and said, "Elizabeth, you are a mess! You smell like ashes, your hair is all tangled, and you are wearing a dirty old paper bag. Come back when you are dressed like a real princess."

"Ronald," said Elizabeth, "your clothes are really pretty and your hair is very neat. You look like a real prince, but you are a bum."

They didn't get married after all.

40 Years of *The Paper Bag Princess*

In 1974, Bob and I were working at the Bay Area Child Care Center in Coos Bay, Oregon. Every day after lunch was naptime for the children. The babies and toddlers were very tired and fell asleep easily, but the older kids—though they didn't mind lying down on cots in the nap room—often didn't calm down enough to fall asleep.

That's when Bob started telling stories. He would begin not knowing where the story would go, and so made it up as he went along. He told stories till all the kids were asleep. He often used some of the kids' own names.

Before long, the kids started asking for particular stories: "Tell us the one about Mortimer!" or "I want to hear the one with the airplane in it." "Tell the one about the fire station!"

He told stories every day. Some were no good. Some he forgot and some got better and better and better. The things the kids liked were kept for the next retelling. These stories didn't even get written down—they lived in his head, or the kids would remind him.

One of the favorite themes involved a prince, a princess, a castle, and a dragon. He told lots and lots of those.

One day, he was telling me about these stories and it struck me that many of the kids in the center were from single-parent homes and had mothers who were doing something really heroic and hard, but in the stories, the hero was always the prince.

"Wait a minute. In your stories, the prince always rescues the princess. Why don't you do something different like have the princess rescue the prince?"

Bob said, "Oh!" And that day at naptime, *The Paper Bag Princess* was born.

Eventually, the parents got to hear some of the stories, and the one where the princess rescues the prince became one of their favorites as well.

Later, at the University of Guelph Preschool, Bob told that story and used the name of a little girl named Elizabeth. When she came to the preschool for the first time she dropped her coat on the floor and waited for Bob to hang it up. He thought, "Wow, this kid really thinks she is a princess!" The name stuck, and after many retellings, the princess was always Elizabeth, and that story became a book.

I like to think that my observation that day in Coos Bay fell on fertile ground. Because Bob is so open to new ideas, so free of preconceptions and bias, he had no knee-jerk reaction that the hero had to be the prince. His way of not being affronted by the idea that the hero of the story could be a girl came from a very deep place. It was and is the part of him that believes kids are important, the same part of him that holds such deep compassion for people just for being what they are—human.

As Bob's career as a storyteller took off, he was always able to count on *The Paper Bag Princess*. It seemed to touch people—they demanded to hear it, they loved to act it out, and audiences were always willing to become part of the story. Even when Bob would ask for a "large, ugly dad" to be the dragon, there were always lots of volunteers! The story resonated with people because it was funny, but it was more than that—audiences loved it because Elizabeth told Ronald off, which surprised people at the time. But Bob knew then, as he still knows today, that everybody—maybe kids especially—always have people in their lives they'd like to stand up to. And by giving the world Elizabeth, he let people know that that was okay.

I like being in a world where *The Paper Bag Princess* lives, and where Elizabeths of all kinds, all over the world, remind us every day that they are our heroes.

Ann Munsch, with Robert Munsch

Even More Classic Munsch

50 Below Zero

Angela's Airplane

The Boy in the Drawer

The Dark

David's Father

The Fire Station

From Far Away

I Have to Go!

Jonathan Cleaned Up—Then He Heard a Sound

Millicent and the Wind

Moira's Birthday

Mortimer

Mud Puddle

Murmel, Murmel, Murmel

Pigs

A Promise is a Promise

Purple, Green and Yellow

Show and Tell

Something Good

Stephanie's Ponytail

Thomas' Snowsuit

Wait and See

Where is Gah-Ning?

Munschworks: The First Munsch Collection

Munschworks 2: The Second Munsch Treasury

Munschworks 3: The Third Munsch Treasury

Munschworks 4: The Fourth Munsch Treasury

The Munschworks Grand Treasury

Munsch Mini-Treasury One

Munsch Mini-Treasury Two

Munsch Mini-Treasury Three

Classic Munsch ABC

Classic Munsch 123

Classic Munsch Moods

For information on these titles please visit www.annickpress.com.
Many Munsch titles are available in French and/or Spanish, as well as in
board book and e-book editions. Please contact your favorite supplier.